GIVE IT A TRY

YASMIN!

written by
SAADIA FARUQI

illustrated by
HATEM ALY

PICTURE WINDOW BOOKS
a capstone imprint

To Mariam for inspiring me,
and Mubashir for helping me find
the right words —S.F.

To my sister, Eman, and her amazing
girls, Jana and Kenzi —H.A.

Yasmin is published by Picture Window Books, an imprint of Capstone.
1710 Roe Crest Drive
North Mankato, Minnesota 56003
www.capstonepub.com

Text copyright © 2021 by Saadia Faruqi.
Illustrations copyright © 2021 by Capstone.

Library of Congress Cataloging-in-Publication Data is available on the Library of Congress website.

ISBN: 978-1-51588-394-4 (paperback)
ISBN: 978-1-51589-199-4 (eBook PDF)

Summary: Yasmin tackles every challenge she faces with her head and her heart. Whether she's helping to solve a recycling problem at school, trying to avoid a science fair fiasco, searching for a favorite lost book, or gathering her courage to join in the fun, Yasmin is always willing to give it a try!

Design Elements:
Shutterstock: LiukasArt, design element

Printed and bound in the USA. PO 3837

TABLE OF CONTENTS

CHAPTER 1

The Helper

Yasmin's class lined up to go to the library. It was the last hour of the day. Everyone was tired.

Except for Yasmin. She was excited. She had a book to show the librarian. And it was her day to be helper!

"Come in, come in!" called Mrs. Kogo, the librarian. "The library is waiting for you!"

The library was big and sunny. There were shelves of books everywhere.

"Yasmin, what's that under your arm?" Mrs. Kogo asked.

"I brought my favorite book to show you. It's about cats. My baba gave it to me!" Yasmin said.

Mrs. Kogo's desk was piled high with books.

"How nice! We'll look at it after our library work is done."

She smiled at Yasmin.

"I see that you're my helper today. If we work together, we can put all the books back in no time!"

Yasmin nodded. "I'm ready to work!"

Busy with Books

Mrs. Kogo showed Yasmin how to shelve books.

"The storybooks go in order by the author's last name," Mrs. Kogo said. She showed Yasmin the alphabet signs on the shelves. "As long as you know your ABCs, you'll be fine."

Yasmin piled all the books in a cart and began shelving. A, then B, then C . . . all the way to Z. She even found an author with the last name Ahmad, just like her!

Emma walked up. "Yasmin, I can't find the book I want," she complained.

Yasmin checked the author's last name. It started with a G.

"Right there!" Yasmin pointed.

"Thanks, Yasmin!" Emma said.

When the books were all shelved, Mrs. Kogo asked Yasmin to tidy up the tables and chairs.

Ali needed help too.

"Yasmin, do you know where the bookmarks are?" he asked.

Yasmin found the box on Mrs. Kogo's desk. "Here you go!"

Finally, all Yasmin's tasks were finished. Now she could show Mrs. Kogo her special book.

But . . . where was it? Yasmin realized she didn't have it anymore.

"My kitaab!" She felt like crying. Where was her book from Baba?

CHAPTER 3

The Special Book

Yasmin took a deep breath and looked around. She'd worked in so many places in the library. How would she find her book? She would have to go back to each one and look.

First, she went to Mrs. Kogo's
desk. The box of bookmarks was
there, but no special book.

Then she went to the shelves. She
checked each section, A through Z.
No special book there, either.

Oh no! Had someone accidentally taken it?

Soon Yasmin heard Mrs. Kogo's

voice. She was talking about animals.

Yasmin turned. Her class was sitting on the carpet. Story time had started. Mrs. Kogo was reading Yasmin's special book from Baba!

She hurried toward them and found a seat next to Emma.

"Yasmin, this book is fantastic," Emma whispered. "Cats are so cool!"

"I know," Yasmin whispered back with a smile.

Then the bell rang. Mrs. Kogo stopped reading. "Thank you for sharing this book with the class, Yasmin!"

"But we didn't get to finish it!" Ali said.

"I have an idea," Yasmin said. "I'll let Mrs. Kogo borrow my book for the week. Then everyone will have a chance to read it!"

Mrs. Kogo smiled. "You make a great librarian, Yasmin!"

CHAPTER 1

Science News

Ms. Alex had finished the science lesson. "Remember, the science fair is next week," she said.

The science fair? Yasmin had forgotten all about it!

"What do we make?" Yasmin whispered to Ali.

"Anything we like!" Ali said.

That wasn't very helpful! Coming up with an idea was hard. What if Yasmin couldn't think of one?

Ms. Alex heard them. "Don't worry, Yasmin. You'll think of something," she said. "After all, science is all around us. Outside. In our classroom. Even in our kitchens!"

"Like when Mama cooks dinner?" Yasmin asked.

Ms. Alex smiled. "Yes. Cooking is also science!"

After school, Yasmin asked Mama, "What should I make for the science fair?"

Mama was busy in the kitchen. "Ideas are everywhere, jaan!"

Not helpful!

Soon Baba came home from work.

"Baba, I need an idea for the science fair," Yasmin said.

"I made an erupting volcano

when I was your age," he said. "It

was fantastic!"

A Volcano Mess

Baba showed Yasmin videos of kids making volcanoes. Some volcanoes were big and tall. Others were short and colorful. All of them made a mess.

"Science is messy," Yasmin complained.

Baba nodded. "Sometimes *learning* is messy, jaan!" he said. "Don't worry."

On Saturday, Baba and Yasmin gathered supplies. Clay from Yasmin's room. Vinegar and baking soda from the kitchen.

"Would you like me to help you?" Baba asked Yasmin.

"I want to try this by myself," Yasmin said.

Baba patted her shoulder.

"I'll be in the living room if you need me," he said.

Yasmin read the instructions they had printed. Then she got to work on her volcano.

Her first try didn't look anything
like a volcano.

On her second try, there were no
bubbles.

On her third try, she spilled
vinegar everywhere. Her volcano was
a mess! Yasmin stomped her foot.
What was she going to do?

Nani entered the kitchen. "How about a lemonade break?" she asked.

Yasmin nodded. All this science had made her thirsty!

Nani squeezed the lemons. She got out the sugar cubes for her tea.

Yasmin loved sugar cubes! She popped one into her mouth. She rolled two cubes like dice on the table. They landed in some spilled baking soda.

Nani poured the lemonade. Yasmin put the two sugar cubes into her glass.

Fizz! The lemonade popped and bubbled. Yasmin gasped. "My lemonade is erupting!"

CHAPTER 3

A Delicious Experiment

It was the day of the science fair.
Yasmin got to school early.

"What will you be presenting, Yasmin?" Ms. Alex asked.

Yasmin held up a big bottle.

"Everyone gets a cup of lemonade!" she said proudly.

Ali looked confused. "That's not a science project!"

"You'll see," Yasmin replied.

The students began to set up their projects. Everyone was excited to present them. Emma had grown beans in a jar. Ali was floating eggs in water.

Ms. Alex and Principal Nguyen took notes on each one.

Soon it was Yasmin's turn. First she lined up the paper cups. Then she poured the lemonade. Next she dropped in the sugar cubes. Finally, Yasmin stirred a little baking soda into each cup.

Pop! Bubble! Fizz! Everyone clapped.

"Amazing!" Ms. Alex said.

"Clever!" Principal Nguyen said.

"It's an erupting volcano—without the mess!" Yasmin said with a grin. "And delicious!"

CHAPTER 1

Something New at School

One Monday, Principal Nguyen held an assembly. "Our school is starting a new recycling program!" he announced.

"I hope that doesn't mean more homework," Ali whispered.

"Shh," Yasmin whispered back.

Principal Nguyen explained. "Factories can make new things out of old things we no longer need. That is recycling. It's one way to help clean up our planet."

He showed the students a symbol with three arrows.

"This symbol means an item can be recycled. Starting tomorrow, the whole school will collect plastic and metal items for recycling."

"Hooray!" Yasmin said. "I want to

help make the planet clean!"

"I just want lunch!" said Ali.

Emma yawned.

CHAPTER 2

A Difficult Job

The next day, there were big green bins around the school.

"We're going to be the best recyclers!" Yasmin said at lunch.

Emma peered into Yasmin's lunch box.

"You brought parathas! Can I have one?" Emma asked.

"Of course!" Yasmin said.

"Can I try?" Ali asked.

Yasmin handed him one too.

Ali took a big bite. "That's delicious! I would do anything for more of those!" he said.

Ali finished his lunch and headed for the bins.

"Don't forget to recycle!" Yasmin said.

"Oh yeah," Ali said. He tossed his water bottle toward the bins.

"Two points!" he yelled.

But the bottle landed in the blue trash bin, *not* the green recycling bin.

"No points!" Yasmin called after him. But Ali didn't hear her.

Principal Nguyen appeared.

"I need some helpers to sort the recycling," he said.

Yasmin stood up. "We'll help!"

Emma shook her head. "Sorry. I have to finish my math."

"But the planet . . . ," Yasmin mumbled.

Didn't her friends want to help?

Yasmin stayed to help the principal. She was sad to see that many kids hadn't put things in the right bins. Plastic items were in the trash. Trash was in the recycling. It was a big mess!

The principal sighed. "The students need encouragement to recycle more. Maybe a party for the class that recycles the most?" he said.

Yasmin thought about her friends at lunch. She smiled. "How about a paratha party? I could ask my mama to help!"

"Delicious idea, Yasmin!" Principal Nguyen said. "Let's go call her together."

CHAPTER 3

A Delicious Prize

Yasmin's mama agreed to make parathas for the party. Yasmin couldn't wait to tell her friends during free time!

"Let's make posters to let everyone know," suggested their teacher, Ms. Alex.

"I'll help!" Emma said.

They got out markers and paper.
When they were done, Yasmin asked
Ali to help hang the posters.

Ali held one up. "A paratha
party?" he said. "Now *I love*
recycling!"

Yasmin beamed.

Ms. Alex's students brought recycling all week. Yasmin brought empty soap bottles. Emma brought cans her family had collected.

Ali brought in the biggest bag of all. Cans, jugs, and all kinds of bottles!

"We can recycle them all. I looked for the symbol!" Ali said.

Soon the green bins were full.

On Friday, Principal Nguyen held another assembly.

"Great job recycling, students!" he said. "The winner is . . . Ms. Alex's class!"

Everyone cheered.

That afternoon, Yasmin's mama and Nani delivered lots of parathas to Ms. Alex's room for the party.

"Helping the planet is great!" said

Yasmin.

"So are parathas!" Ali said, and

he took a big bite.

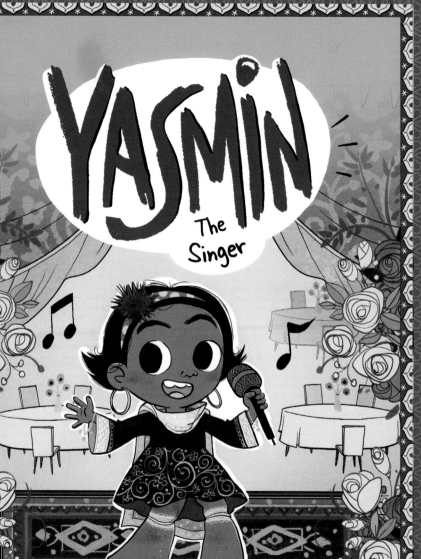

A Party

It was a very special evening. Yasmin, Mama, and Nani were going to a party.

Yasmin loved wearing her Pakistani shalwar kameez.

"You look wonderful!" Baba exclaimed.

"Thank you," Yasmin replied.

"I think he's talking to me, jaan!"
Nani teased.

The party was at Aunt Zara's
house. Her friend was getting married.

"Salaam!" Aunt Zara said. "You're
going to have so much fun, Yasmin!"

Yasmin felt shy as they entered the
house.

There were so many people in
the room. Their clothes were colorful.
Their jewelry sparkled.

The bride was dressed in the most beautiful clothes. Yasmin couldn't stop staring at her.

Mama talked with Aunt Zara. Then she pointed to a woman sitting across the room.

"Want to put on some henna, Yasmin?" Mama asked.

"Will you come with me?" Yasmin asked.

Mama nodded.

The woman painted a pretty design on Yasmin's hand.

"It matches my dress, Mama," Yasmin whispered.

Mama smiled. "It certainly does!"

They ate delicious food and
walked around the room.

"Why don't you go play with the
kids?" Mama suggested.

Yasmin shook her head. She
wanted to stay close to Mama.

CHAPTER 2

Sing a Song with Me

After dinner, a group of girls sat on the floor. They played a dholki and clapped their hands. They laughed and sang songs in Urdu with happy voices.

The other guests sat around them, listening. Smiling.

Mama knew the words to the song. "You know this one too, Yasmin. Sing with us!"

"No, thanks," Yasmin mumbled.

She felt like everyone was looking at her.

Yasmin got up and walked quietly
to the side of the room. She just
wanted to be alone.

Nani waved to her. "Come here, jaan," she called. But Yasmin shook her head. She was just fine in the corner.

Next to her was a pretty silk curtain. Yasmin slid behind it and sat down.

That was better! Now nobody could see her. Yasmin listened to the song and felt her heart jump. Mama was right. She did know this one!

Soon, Yasmin was singing too. It was just a whisper, but that was okay. She sang softly, just to herself. It made her happy. It was a song about a bride, about beautiful clothes, and about henna.

Yasmin sang and sang.

CHAPTER 3

An Audience

Yasmin's voice got louder. She stood up. She imagined she was on a stage. The music was all around her, happy and loud.

She struck a pose. She flipped her head. She held up a pretend microphone.

Yasmin was so busy singing, she didn't see what she was doing. Her arm caught in the curtain. Before she could catch it, the curtain dropped to the floor.

Yasmin turned around. She stopped singing. Everyone in the room was looking at her.

"Oops," she whispered.

The girls on the floor were still drumming on the dholki, but they weren't singing.

They were all watching Yasmin. And they were all smiling. Then they started to clap!

Mama and Nani were smiling too.

Mama walked up and held out her hand.

"Your voice is lovely, jaan. Come join us. Let's sing together!"

Yasmin took Mama's hand. It was okay. She was ready to sing with the others.

Think About It, Talk About It

* What special item might you take to school for show-and-tell or to share with a friend or teacher? Why is it special to you?

* If you could be in a science fair, what project would you present?

* Does your school have a recycling program? If not, write a letter to your principal asking if you could start one.

* Have you been to a special party or event where you got to dress up? If you could wear whatever you wanted, what would it be? Draw a picture.

Learn Urdu with Yasmin!

Yasmin's family speaks both English and Urdu. Urdu is a language from Pakistan. Maybe you already know some Urdu words!

baba (BAH-bah)—father

dholki (DOL-kee)—a two-headed drum used with traditional Pakistani songs

henna (HEN-ah)—red or brown dye used to draw designs on the skin that will fade away

jaan (jahn)—life; a sweet nickname for a loved one

kameez (kuh-MEEZ)—long tunic or shirt

kitaab (kee-TAHB)—book

nani (NAH-nee)—grandmother on mother's side

salaam (sah-LAHM)—hello

shalwar (shahl-WAHR)—loose trousers worn under a kameez

Pakistan Fun Facts

Yasmin and her family are proud of their Pakistani culture. Yasmin loves to share facts about Pakistan!

Islamabad

Pakistan is on the continent of Asia, with India on one side and Afghanistan on the other.

The word Pakistan means "land of the pure" in Urdu and Persian.

Many languages are spoken in Pakistan, including Urdu, English, Saraiki, Punjabi, Pashto, Sindhi, and Balochi.

The word paratha means layers of cooked dough. Paratha is often served with butter, pickles, or other toppings.

Pakistan started a program called Clean Green Pakistan in 2018 to help improve the country's environment.

Make a Recycle Monster

SUPPLIES:

- 2 large brown paper bags
- markers
- scissors
- tape

STEPS:

1. Turn one paper bag up upside down. On the front, draw eyes, a nose, and a big open mouth—big enough to fit bottles and cans through.

2. Cut out the mouth so there is an opening in the middle of the bag.

3. Lay down the second bag right side up and write FEED ME! on it.

4. Draw the recycle symbol underneath the words.

5. Place the first bag over the opening of the second and tape the two open sides together.

6. Place your Recycle Monster in your room, kitchen, or classroom, and feed it recycling!

About the Author

Saadia Faruqi is a Pakistani American writer, interfaith activist, and cultural sensitivity trainer featured in *O Magazine*. She is author of two middle grade novels, *A Place at the Table* and *A Thousand Questions*. She is also editor-in-chief of *Blue Minaret*, an online magazine of poetry, short stories, and art. Besides writing books, she also loves reading, binge-watching her favorite shows, and taking naps. She lives in Houston, Texas, with her husband and children.

About the Illustrator

Hatem Aly is an Egyptian-born illustrator whose work has been published all over the world. He currently lives in beautiful New Brunswick, Canada, with his wife, son, and more pets than people. When he is not dipping cookies in a cup of tea or staring at blank pieces of paper, he is usually drawing, reading, or daydreaming. You can see his art in books that earned multiple starred reviews and positions on the *NYT* Best-Sellers list, such as *The Proudest Blue* (with Ibtihaj Muhammad & S.K. Ali) and *The Inquisitor's Tale* (with Adam Gidwitz), a Newbery Honor winner.